good deed rain

48 Books by Allen Frost

...Ohio Trio...Bowl of Water...
...Another Life...Home Recordings...
...The Mermaid Translation...The Selected
Correspondence of Kenneth Patchen...
...The Wonderful Stupid Man...
...Saint Lemonade...Playground...Roosevelt...
...5 Novels...The Sylvan Moore Show...
...Town in a Cloud...A Flutter of Birds
Passing Through Heaven: A Tribute to Robert
Sund.......At the Edge of America.......
....Lake Erie Submarine....The Book of Ticks....
.........I Can Only Imagine.........
...The Orphanage of Abandoned Teenagers...
...Different Planet...Go With the Flow: A
Tribute to Clyde Sanborn...Homeless Sutra...
..The Lake Walker..A Hundred Dreams Ago..
....Almost Animals....The Robotic Age....
....Kennedy....Fable....Elbows & Knees:
Essays and Plays....The Last Paper Stars....
...Walt Amherst is Awake...When You Smile
You Let in Light....Pinocchio in America....
....Florida....Blue Anthem Wailing....
...The Welfare Office...Island Air...
...Imaginary Someone...Violet of the Silent
Movies....The Tin Can Telephone....
....Heaven Crayon....Old Salt....
...A Field of Cabbages...River Road...
....The Puttering Marvel....
..Something Bright...The Trillium Witch...
..Cosmonaut..

COSMONAUT

COSMONAUT © 2021
Allen Frost, Good Deed Rain
Bellingham, Washington
ISBN 978-1-0878-9431-7

Writing: Allen Frost
Cover Art: Laura Vasyutynska
Interior Drawings: Allen Frost
Cover Production: Katrina Svoboda
Apple: TFK!

Credits:
Movie quote from *The 7th Victim*, RKO Radio Pictures, 1943.
John Coltrane quote from *Down Beat*, April 12, 1962.
Yuri Gagarin, *Road to the Stars,* Foreign Languages Publishing House, 1962.
Movie newspaper headline appeared in *Warning From Space*, Daiei Film, 1956.

"Blessed are you, because the sight of me
does not disturb you."

—*The Gospel of Mary Magdalene*

C O S M O N A U T

Allen Frost

Good Deed Rain ◊ Bellingham, Washington ◊ 2021

For Gianni Rodari

"The time is out of tune."

—*The 7th Victim*

"Music is just a reflection of the universe, like life in miniature."

—John Coltrane

"The noise was no louder than one would expect to hear in a jet plane, but it had a great range of musical tones and timbres that no composer could hope to score, and no musical instrument or human voice could ever reproduce."

—Yuri Gagarin

the CHAPTERS

I.
WELCOME to EARTH

Cornelius Barter was in his backyard. It was after 2 AM. He sat in a chair with his head back, his eyes glassed over with stars. He was so motionless he could have been a scarecrow. Another airplane blinked across the wide sky. It left a streak in the air like a telephone wire.

Then something else caught Barter's attention. A silver light inched out from the stars. He watched it for ten seconds before he finally moved in his chair. Nobody else noticed it fall.

It kept falling, getting closer, an orange glow around it now. It looked like a car meteor—that's what came to Barter's mind—an Oldsmobile shot out of a circus cannon.

Whoever was driving it was steering right for the treed-in dead end of Elwood Avenue where Cornelius sat in his chair. There was already one abandoned car sunk in the wave of blackberry spilling over the fence from the woods, and now it looked like another was on the way. Cornelius almost managed to sit up. The back of his legs pushed against the trumpet case. No matter what, his trumpet was never far. After years he trained himself to keep it near like a faithful dog.

The falling star, or whatever it was, continued

straight down then leveled, just missing the black shadowy trees by the creek. Cornelius covered his eyes with his hand and looked through a gap in his fingers. Most people would have been running for cover. Cornelius Barter was slow to react to everything except when he was playing music. Then he was in a world of his own making. The minute he strayed from that path though, he was lost.

If Yuri Gagarin's space capsule had been ten feet to the left, this book would be over. Or at least it would be different. It would begin with the explosion of a Sputnik crashlanding into a jazz musician. The *Herald* would send a reporter and maybe this book would be that story. Espionage, invasion, Cold War, music in underground clubs. Soundtrack by Cornelius Barter.

With a sudden crash, the little trailer was crushed like a stomped tin can.

Finally, Cornelius was on his feet. The dust was settling.

His house was flat as a vinyl LP. Music always came first. He thought of all his records, smashed. Lester Young and Paul Desmond were gone with the wind.

A scarred, burnt up spacecraft sat in the middle of the litter where his trailer used to be. Then it was covered by a descending parachute. A red parachute. Thanks to the feeble light of the streetlamp on the sidewalk he could read the four letters repeating around the cloth: CCCP.

Cornelius thought maybe this was a dream. If he wanted to, he could wake himself up. It felt like the only time he wasn't in a dream was when he played. But that could be a dream too, couldn't it? In that case, everything was a dream.

Metal scratched. Behind the parachute cloth the ship's door was opening. It was having a hard time, it fought like a big fish caught in a net. It pushed and shoved until Cornelius reached down and lifted the edge of parachute, pulling the ropes out of the way too. He didn't know what or who to expect—Nikita Khrushchev could have landed in his backyard.

Yuri Gagarin climbed out into the night air. He dropped to the tin covered ground. He couldn't see much through his helmet shield. It was the dead of night in America. The green lights from his capsule shined into the dark and dimly lit the shape of a person greeting him. Gagarin was taught at Military Unit 26266 in Star City to be prepared for unwelcome natives. His thick gloves could turn into fists if necessary. But it was okay.

Cornelius raised a hand like someone holding a flower. He was saying something too.

This was Yuri's welcome back to Earth. He removed his helmet so he could hear. The first breath of this world's air rushed him like the incoming tide and he almost fell. How long had it been? Years. There was that famous smile you saw on the front page of Pravda. He missed Russia—he was off by an ocean—but he had finally returned to his home planet.

"You a spaceman?" Cornelius asked. It was a good guess.

Unfortunately, Yuri didn't understand English. It had been so long, he wondered if he would understand Russian when he heard it again. His thoughts might be in a whole other language by now. These words he was greeted with sounded like something poured from a rusted horn.

"You…You really smashed up my house," said Cornelius. He looked at the remains of Miles Davis' *Blue Period* record by his shoe. It had scattered free of the crater as far as it could. Oh, he thought, what can you do when something like this happens? His record player and those albums he loved were gone. So was his bed, his kitchen, his awards and his duffel of clothes… the radio…whatever it was that he carried with him when he went from gig to gig. He telegrammed his hand to make sure it held the trumpet case. That was what mattered most.

Yuri tried to say something, but curiously he wasn't able to speak. It was strange, as if he was underwater and he just didn't dare try. The helmet made him feel like he was in an aquarium, and even if he wasn't wearing it, after all the places he had been, he was floating, only floating after all.

Cornelius wondered what he could do to make a cosmonaut feel at home. He had some money in his pocket and he knew Rocket Market stayed open all night. It didn't seem to matter that Yuri was wearing a bright orange spacesuit, people at this hour were mostly in dreams. They could walk to the store and be back in ten minutes. By the fence was another chair. They could sit and look up at the stars and when night was done it would be morning. Sure, Cornelius figured, then his visitor could see the territory tomorrow.

After putting his helmet back in the ship and securing the hatch, Yuri was ready. He had done this before on other planets.

"You hungry?" asked Cornelius. He guessed he was. Rocket Market would have something that might be a step above space rations. Cornelius wished he knew some Russian. He could say thank you, "Spasiba," that's it. He tried to send a telepathic message and was not surprised when it seemed to be working.

Yuri smiled and walked with him.

They were both leaving the yard. The orange streetlamp sparkled on the rough tar, making little stars on the road. Cornelius decided to keep talking, after a while maybe the spaceman would be able to decode him. "There's a store not far from here."

Yuri wanted to say something, he wanted to ask Cornelius Barter why he was carrying a trumpet case. Gagarin liked the trumpet, he learned to play one in Saratov Industrial Technical School. He hoped this was one of those American jazz musicians he could hear drifting on the Voice of America. It was forbidden to listen to, but you couldn't stop airwaves. Under the trees, the sound of his suit walking brushed like a snare drum playing with Billie Holiday.

They cut across the street over the sidewalk until Cornelius turned into the weeds. The path seemed to glow in the darkness. It was easy to follow. Like a shadowy stream, it led them into a wooded glen. Yuri had to stop. He put both hands on the alder and held its slim waist.

Cornelius stopped just ahead, and turned and said, "Uhhh…"

From the shadows Yuri's smile was wide as the Cheshire Cat. He patted the tree and motioned his hands around at the canopy of nighttime leaves. He breathed deeply and clenched his gloves. This place reminded him of the trees bordering the village farm. In fact, he could hear a creek nearby, and just ahead of them, past the trees, was a field big as a lake under the moonlight.

Nodding, Cornelius understood the feeling: he felt the same way leaving Oklahoma. He remembered stepping off the bus in California and hugging the first palm tree he saw. All he owned was a suitcase and his trumpet and he was only blocks from Charlie Parker.

Yuri's smile hadn't left.

Cornelius noticed that Yuri was looking past the trees to a band of tall grass in the nearby field. "Listen to this." Cornelius unlatched the trumpet case. He fit it with the mouthpiece and pointed it towards the field and played a few lullaby notes. They were still hanging in the air as another sound joined in and echoed from hiding places around them. Coyotes were howling and crying. Now it was Cornelius smiling. "Isn't that something?"

Sometimes at night in Klushino, that same eerie rippling cracked the air.

Cornelius stowed his trumpet and they started walking again. A few coyotes continued to screech. It was hard to think that was an earthly song, but it was. The path split and would have brought them into the field if they followed that branch. Instead, they went the other way, along the trees, over a wooden plank bridge then uphill. A faint light smudged the branches up there. That light became the smoldering red and green neon of the Rocket Market rooftop.

The path broke and spilled them out onto the pavement. One car was parked next to the store. It was waiting for the night shift to end. Big yellow store windows shined on the side of the car, glazing it. Up high, the sign buzzed. It was a tone familiar to Yuri: the capsule's shortwave radio would bristle like that between terrestrial broadcasts. Over the ocean, the circuits would fizz.

Cornelius held the door open for his companion and Yuri walked into his first American convenience store. He would have been a strange sight in most places. Not at 2 A.M.

The cashier was used to the night people, they were a whole other crowd, separate from sunshine. This hour belonged to interplanetary visitors. As the door chimed and closed, Benton watched his two customers in the mirror, from the safety of his boxed-in counter space. His foot slid a little on the linoleum. A button on the floor connected him to the police. Then his foot froze. Benton had seen Cornelius before, he was a character known around town, but why was Benton's parole officer walking with him? Benton tried to hide behind the wall of cigarettes.

"Good evening," Cornelius said. The radio was playing and for a second he caught himself in it. Then he almost bumped into the cosmonaut standing in front of him. Yuri was frozen, dazzled by the lights and aisles of shelves.

In outer space, far past Mars, there's a convenience store like this, floating like a lily pad. When Yuri coasted his Vostok onto the platform and parked and went inside, he felt this same way.

"You hungry?" Cornelius asked him. "You see anything you want?"

II.

The WONDERS of MORE than ONE WORLD

They walked back along the street instead of the way they arrived. Cornelius explained, "Those coyotes might be hungry too." Yuri held a paper plate with five hamburgers. Five were already gone.

Rocket Market never sold ten to one person before. It was a record. Still, something wasn't quite right about it, Benton felt something unreal was happening. The temperature dropped as they left the counter and eddied along in a cold breeze. The nightshift was full of strange events like this. In a few hours the sun would appear, washing away the dream.

It should have been a peaceful return to the backyard—they were only blocks away—but a neighborhood errand in the middle of the night can easily become a journey into the unknown. That's how they got noticed on the wrong radar and where their trouble really began. (Then again, if it didn't begin here, it would have been somewhere else sooner or later).

"Oh no…" Cornelius sighed. He pointed at the silhouette figure kneeling beside a dark car. A flashlight clicked and illuminated a man holding a tire gauge next to the whitewall. After checking the air, he popped up and positioned the flashlight under his arm so he could write a note. With the air of a traffic cop, he tore the page out of his little book and slipped the warning under the windshield wiper. Cornelius couldn't believe it…It was just their luck that the road ran into Pestus Cleek.

The flashlight circle danced their way and Cornelius held a protective hand over his eyes.

"That you, Mr. Barter?"

"Cleek…" Cornelius replied.

"Who's that with you?"

Yuri Gagarin shielded his eyes with a half-eaten hamburger. He was relieved when the light went out. He was waiting for another bite.

"Just me and my friend strolling."

"Strolling…" Cleek considered, "A little late for strolling I would have thought. But I guess that's life for a jazz musician. As for me, my job never ends. The owner of this vehicle will be glad I alerted them to add some air to their tire. Say—" like a cartoon character with a sudden idea, the light bulb flicked again, flashing on Yuri, "Is that a spacesuit?" Before either of them could respond, Cleek reasoned, "Quite realistic. You were probably at a masquerade ball."

"That's right."

The light went out. It was a miracle Cleek didn't spot Yuri's space capsule descending. He must have been busy snooping in a flowerbed or measuring someone's lawn with a tape measure.

But Cornelius didn't want to push their luck, he didn't like the suspicious shadowy look that regarded them still. You could boil that shadow for an hour and it wouldn't soften. It was always that way when he ran into Cleek—the guy was always looking for treachery. So, Cornelius was quick to cut their conversation short and say goodbye. If Cleek suspected a Russian had landed in their neighborhood there would be pandemonium.

Yuri didn't mind. He was glad to be part of it, on a sidewalk in a pleasant late evening, hamburgers, and a cold bottle of Coca-Cola zippered in his lining. A row of big American houses slept like whales on grassy seas. Each driveway held a car fitted with chrome, ready to go.

Silent as a memory of Kitty Hawk, an owl soared overhead, aimed like a glider for the woods. Yuri watched its flight. He had been to a small planet ruled by owls and he spent some time with them. They wore their wings like capes and talked to him from trees. The forest always stayed a murky blue and he spent hours lying on the moss and listening to them. He stayed long enough to learn their language and he wanted to call back to that Earth owl, but his mouth was full.

The rest of the way to the crooked fence that

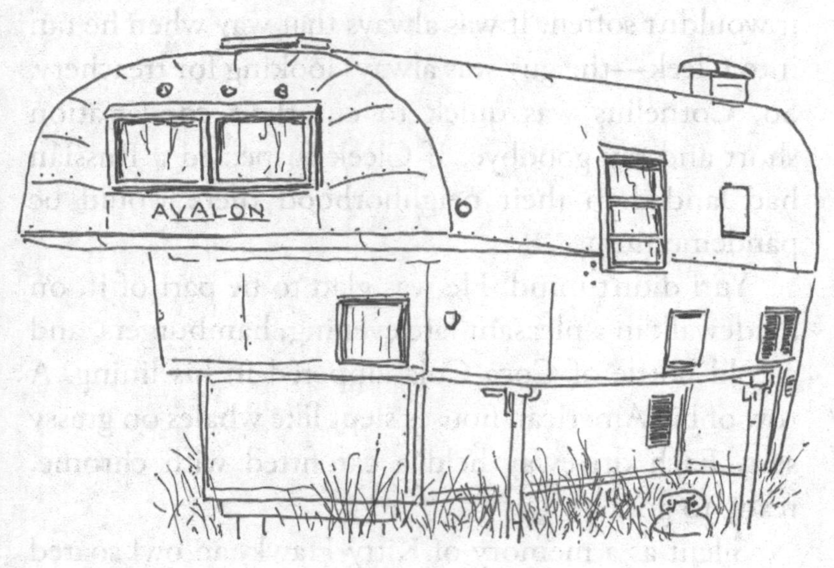

in a calm pool of night

bordered Cornelius Barter's yard was like a studio when the music is done and the lights are out except for a glow on the monitor board. Sometimes Cornelius would sit against the wall in that padded room and he could still hear the last note long after it was gone.

Every uneven slat of the wooden fence leaned like piano keys. Later in the summer it was lined by tall grasses and tangled morning glory. Spring was only beginning. Those flowers were still on their voyage back.

The gate was kept shut by a knotted string of rope, only now it was dangling. They must have left it that way when they left. Either that or a coyote let itself in. Cornelius wasn't the only one who liked to sit in a chair by starlight.

Just an hour ago, that chair was here in a weedy lot with a trailer, in a calm pool of night. The owner of The Moon Bird let Cornelius stay rent-free for as long as he played at the club. What a benefit, there weren't many gigs like that. Cornelius let a month go by, jazz until 2, then home to a trailer not much bigger than the spaceship that laid it flat. It all ended so fast. The air still smelled like a blown-out candle.

Yuri was used to being in the dark, pressing switches and reading dials, but after all those hamburgers he was tired and he yawned. There was mustard on his glove.

"Yeah, well...Sorry I can't offer you a place to crash." Cornelius gave a short laugh, "All I have now is my trumpet and that chair."

Another yawn and the two of them separated for the night, what was left of it. Cornelius settled back into his chair, the same way he looked before. The only change was the faintest hint of light smudging in the east.

And Yuri Gagarin had crawled under the parachute, into his spacecraft, onto his own chair. A little lamp was on. He kept the hatch open. There were planets he had been to where he wouldn't do that—just think of those giant mosquitoes on BXE13M. They dressed as encyclopedia salesmen and knocked on the door and promised him the wonders of their world for just 50 rubles a month, and the first volume was free! It was a good deal, but he managed to resist their pitch.

Even though sleep was perched on the armrest, ready to take his arm and run him into dreams, he resisted. He reached into a compartment beneath the console and got his logbook. Those mosquitoes of BXE13M could buzz all they wanted, he was filling this book with the wonders of more than one world. This book was his company. He could open it up and remember instantly. Like the time he landed on HTO5J. That took some expert piloting to land on the only spot that wasn't water. Retrorockets and a black smoke roar made the fish scatter. Then he eased the rocket onto the one hill that rose from the sea. If you've watched any cartoons like this, or read fairy tales, you would know what to expect. But they didn't cover that at the Cosmonaut Training Center. He had no way of knowing that hill was the back of a whale. Or was it a fish the size of a whale? More likely it was an entirely different classification of creature. He didn't stay long enough to find out, he had to restart the rockets and hurry from there. From the porthole window, he could see that hill sink completely into the waves. That encounter was written in his logbook. If anyone else went to HTO5J, they wouldn't make that mistake. At the end of the entry, Yuri wrote: *Bring a boat.*

The log wasn't just a diary of his life in space, it was also a guidebook for those who would come after him. Anywhere he stopped received at least a page, even DP21. What a nightmare. First of all, it was nothing but concrete. Yuri landed near an austere looking building. It could have been home for the Communist Union of Motor Vehicle Licensing Bureau. It turned out it was DP21's answer to that. A very old woman in a gray suit was waiting for Yuri when the smoke cleared. She held a clipboard. It turned out she was a parking meter maid and she wanted to charge him to park there. She held out three hands. "But I'm not staying long," he argued. "Before you know it, I'll be gone." While she was getting her ticket book, he legged it back to the ship. For DP21, Yuri Gagarin simply wrote: *Skip it.*

Outer space was full of dangers and disappointments and vast lonely distance, but fortunately, for every BXE13M, HTO5J, or DP21, there was a SFN88. He couldn't believe such a place existed. He never wanted to leave. It was like when he went to Cuba in 1961, stepping from that Tupolev airliner into the tropics, seven thousand miles from the cold Soviet Union. He took off his helmet right away, removed his orange spacesuit and boots and dug his toes into the sand. For ten days he walked on the beach, slept in a hammock under flowering palms, ate the fruits right off the trees, and caught fish with a bamboo pole. If it wasn't for his duty to the motherland, he could have staged an accident—he could have buried all traces of the Vostok 1 and lived the rest of his life as a castaway.

That didn't happen, he kept traveling. Eventually, he found his way back to Earth. The sound out the round doorway wasn't the gentle surf of SFN88 and he couldn't hear tree frogs or singing moths. He wasn't breathing in the scent of luminous petals. He wondered if he ever would again. Maybe once he crossed the Pacific and delivered his report, the committee would allow him to return to his favorite faraway planet.

A red circle of light shined behind the parachute while he wrote. The pen scratched, stopped, and a bottlecap snitched. What an advertisement for Coca Cola—a cosmonaut in America, listening to Lee Konitz on his short-wave radio while he drinks coke. Yuri Gagarin would toast the glory of the free world.

Thirty feet away a chair was pulled up under the fading night and pointed west. Cornelius Barter was tired too. His face was blank as a mask. He already had his Green 17. His eyes had opened doors where they were seeing another world. Every once in a while he would take a breath and let it go, otherwise you would never know this wasn't Cornelius Barter in the wax museum. The morning light was crawling slowly on its way. His trumpet lay on his lap like a sleeping cat.

III.

The BALLAD of PESTUS CLEEK

Pestus Cleek was there at sunrise. He had a feeling there was something funny about that spaceman and after a few hours that feeling became an ominous premonition. True, on more than one occasion his suspicions got him in trouble—like the time he found a ticking clock he thought was a bomb buried in a garbage can, or when he mistook a stray dog for a prowler, or the evening he scared Mrs. Raymond when he appeared at her window like Lon Chaney—but those other times were easily forgotten as he got his binoculars focused. He steadied his elbows on the fence. The cherry tree branch above him held its breath. And then he gasped…What he caught in sight was more than he ever dreamed. All those days and nights pacing the neighborhood…No prayer he ever made and waited for arrived with such fanfare.

Cornelius Barter was dead in his chair, and his Russian murderer was folding a parachute next to a sputnik.

This was big—this was bigger than anything Pestus ever imagined on his dark walks. Stranger than *Journey to the Seventh Planet*. He saw that picture twice when it played, but that was nothing compared to this excitement.

Cleek quickly lowered the binoculars and let himself sink behind the fence like a submarine. His lanky knees folded under himself tight as the legs of an old card table. His mind was racing—this could be an invasion! Russians like this one were probably dropping out of the sky all over America. Someone needed to do something, he needed to contact the authorities, the military had to be alerted!

If only Cleek had turned for home and gone to sleep instead. Yuri Gagarin would have spent a couple days exploring, listening to jazz, enjoying his stay until it was time to get into his spaceship and leave. This adventure would be a two-page story in the log. Then one rocket leap would take him across the Pacific Ocean and he would be in Russia.

Pestus Cleek slunk low along the fence. If he could get to Elwood Avenue, he knew the location of the nearest phone booth. He shook along in the weeds like a snake in a hurry.

Yuri looked across the splash of dandelions. On the other side of the fence, he saw something dark rushing away. If this was ZK9, that would be a six-legged newt chasing a cricket the size of a chicken. It ambled that way. He paid it no mind. He had his parachute to fold and reload. Then he had to make his spaceship invisible.

The morning birds were singing from branches.

They greeted every day this way, even if it was raining.

Once Pestus left the last corner of fencing, he straightened up and began to shuffle. He had a panicked look, like an owl trying to outrun the sun. Across the lot of Rocket Market his coattails flapped.

A car parked next to the store was refusing to start. The engine rattled and gasped and stopped until the driver turned the key again.

Ignoring that clatter, Pestus scuffed up to the phone booth. He patted his pockets looking for change. Where was it? Where did he put his coin purse?

From behind him, the car door cracked open and the driver called, "Excuse me," getting outside. Benton didn't mean to startle Pestus, but it wasn't hard to. Cleek was jumpy as a trembling leaf. Every night Pestus Cleek would swing open the Rocket Market door and move like an eel to the candy shelves. "I really shouldn't," he would tell Benton, "I can't resist though," twitching looks over his shoulder. He bought a Mounds bar promptly every 2:15 A.M. Pestus would take his time with it as he made the rounds.

In his surprise, Pestus dropped his coin purse. "What?" he said a little too loud.

One time at the counter, Pestus dropped his Mounds and you would have thought the sky was falling. If only that event was caught on film, Art Linkletter would have had a heyday.

Benton told him, "You should go inside and see Digby." Digby LeStac was on dayshift duty. "He's got—"

"What? I don't have time for that," Cleek almost shouted. "You have no idea what I just saw. We have an emergency."

"Oh."

"And kindly stop trying to start that car for a minute, I have an important call to make." Cleek got a dime out and dropped it in the slot. Of course he knew the phone number for the police. His fingers rolled around the dial.

Benton watched from his car. He heard Pestus Cleek bleat out a crazy story of Russians and jazz murder. He shook his head. Next to him on the seat was a copy of Digby LeStac's latest record. This was happening just like the lyrics.

Pestus hung up and turned around. He looked smug as an admiral in a painting.

So Benton turned the key again and this time his Dodge roared to life. It always started again sooner or later. The engine calmed to a raspy wheeze like a sandbag in a washing machine and the car reversed from the building wall.

Cleek wasn't about to waste his time with Digby right now. Every time he spoke with him, Cleek felt like he was being recorded by an anthropologist.

Digby LeStac was a folk troubadour. Musicians were everywhere. Then Cleek thought of poor Cornelius Barter dead in his chair. Now there was one less song in the air. He walked severely back in the direction he had come. When the police arrived, Pestus Cleek wanted to be there.

He didn't notice the hum coming from Rocket Market as he passed the glass windows. He quickly disappeared off the tarmac with those stork legs of his punching at the air.

Digby LeStac turned the radio up. They were playing his song.

A few streets away, on Madrona, a police car cut the corner with a squeal. The two officers on the front seat leaned into the turn. It was too early for a siren. There were still a few backyard roosters crowing here and there. The driver straightened the wheel and pressed the gas pedal. They knew it wasn't an emergency, they knew they were responding to a Pestus Cleek report— believe it or not, there was even a radio code for that— but not much else was going on at dawn, they had to do something.

The black and white patrol car growled onto Taylor Avenue. It didn't slow until they turned past Flowers Childcare then it swooped onto the gravel shoulder. This was as close as they could get to the scene of the crime. They had to walk the rest of the way there.

Cornelius Barter was no stranger to the police department either. Last month they arrested him for Green 17, and it wouldn't be the last time, they were sure. The fact that he was living in an Airstream trailer a hundred yards away was no secret to them. They had orders to keep their eye on him.

They were a little late though. Cornelius and Yuri had vanished.

What they found, when they looked over that same fence Cleek had fled from, was an empty yard. No sign of the supposed victim or his killer. Even the trailer was gone. Strange…it couldn't have just up and flown away. They studied the rough patchy grass and yellow flowers. No evidence of the trailer rolling out, no tracks left behind. There was nothing to see. But the two officers weren't surprised.

"Looks like Cleek's crying wolf again."

"Yeah."

Birds were singing in the cherry tree. What was going to happen, what were they going to do, arrest a sparrow?

A few minutes after the cops left, those little birds were still singing when Pestus Cleek arrived, out of breath. He didn't see any police yet, no flashing lights, no black bulletproof jackets swarming the path. He was glad he got there before them. In spite of the danger he anticipated, a thin smile scratched his face.

Finally, he sighed, he would be believed. Sadly for him, he wasn't pleased when he looked over the wall.

Birds flew from him, a deer froze, the police car rumbled up the road and his song was spinning on the radio again. It was a hit. The aerial on top the Leopold would be repeating it all day, transmitting a five mile broadcast range for everyone to hear, a pigeon, seagulls, the clouds that slowly edged in across the bay.

IV.
CRACKLING & FLASH

Yuri Gagarin stepped out of the air. Half of him reached back into invisibility where he leaned and picked a stone off the ground. It was no ordinary rock though: it was from Planet YIT812. Held gently as a pear, he carried it ten yards and began to dowse with it until he saw a pattern appear at his feet. Like the tiny bits of gold in a streambed, a path formed. He bent and pressed the stone into the track that had already been scratched into the soil. As he drew the stone around, following the circle, the old easy chair began to slowly reappear. When Yuri came back to the spot where he started, Cornelius was no longer zippered up hidden from sight. He was slumped like a laundry bag.

What would happen if Yuri lost the stone? The same thing that happened when he left YIT812. Those strange creatures that lived there remained invisible, floating in space on a planet that was there but could only be found by accident, only if you bumped into it in your ship like he did. He put the rock safely into one of his orange pockets. If he lost it, his Vostok might as well be a million miles from Earth.

After all the planets he had seen (and not seen) he still found a simple early morning of birds and good clean cool air to be a miracle. He didn't want to rouse Cornelius, but he had to, he was hungry. This was America, this was where people ate mountains of food and never had to stand in lines to get rations. He tried to speak, but maybe after all that time in space he couldn't remember how. He had been alone for so long the words were only thoughts in his head.

With his black boot he gave Barter's chair a push. It tipped and came back onto its springs. Nothing. This guy could sleep through a centrifuge.

Then Yuri remembered being at the store last night, where Cornelius paid with money he kept in his trumpet case. Yuri considered it—he could take just enough for another meal—but it wouldn't do for him to thieve, he wasn't put on planets to steal. He set a gloved hand on Cornelius' shoulder and shook him.

Nothing.

Yuri clapped his gloves loudly. Still no response.

"You won't wake him up that way."

Yuri startled and turned towards the fence. A gray-haired man in a blue windbreaker stared at him. There was nothing that seemed unfriendly about him, Yuri thought. He was right. Mitch Itchmay was a cartoonist. He rode his bicycle around town collecting ideas. He had a notebook in his handlebar basket filled with drawings. *The Sunday Pictorial* featured one every week.

Then Mitch suddenly realized who he was looking at next to Cornelius Barter. "Ms. Parden? I can't believe it!" He laughed. Impossibly, after so many years, he was facing his 7th grade teacher. Because of her, he listened to the Jack Benny Show and Duke Ellington. How wild she was standing in this yard.

Mitch let himself through the gate and pushed his bicycle to a spot against the fence. "Remember you told me I should become an artist? Well, guess what?"

Yuri smiled and waited.

"I'm a successful cartoonist now. I'm published in the newspapers and national journals."

Yuri decided this was a character, every village had one. Mitch wore gray shorts all year long and could often be seen puffing along the streets of town in any kind of weather. "Oh—here's how you wake him up," Mitch said. As he neared, he reached into his coat pocket and Yuri saw him get a metallic toy of some kind. Mitch stopped next to the chair. When he blew into the kazoo, Yuri instantly remembered the geese of CNB558.

The trumpet player stirred, opening glazed eyes. "Hey—hey, Mitch…How are you?"

"Well, for one thing I can't believe who's here with you."

"Ohhh, this is…" Cornelius mumbled, "I guess I don't know his name…He's a spaceman. He showed up in that—" he pushed himself around in his chair, but he didn't see that capsule on the remains of his trailer. There was only grass where they had been. "What?"

Mitch Itchmay had seen Cornelius like this before. He knew to just play it cool.

Yuri could read his comrade's confusion. He wished he could explain. He could show them the stone from YIT812 and give them a demonstration of the vanishing act. That was a little risky though. People still believed in witchcraft.

"You ready to go to breakfast?" Mitch asked.

"Right..." Cornelius held the armrests. "I forgot." He reached for his trumpet case and then stood up. He didn't remember anything about breakfast plans. He never had breakfast, usually he slept til the afternoon. What happened last night? He recalled being at The Moon Bird, playing "Time After Time." The band took five and he took Green 17 to a cloud. Oh, it must have been then—Mitch was at the gig.

The three of them made an odd assortment walking along the forested path. They could have starred on the screen of the Peoples Theatre. *The Man from Planet X* could be the second feature. Mitch pushed his bike with one hand while his other hand directed his storytelling. His arm moved like a painter. Cornelius and Yuri listened. They both looked like they were listening to a long-playing record. Once Mitch got started, he liked to talk. Fortunately, their breakfast wasn't far.

The Tin Goose Diner sat in a parking lot with its wings spread over the cars. It was an old Ford Tri-Motor airliner that had been transformed into a café. Seeing it, Yuri grinned and clapped his gloves together. He hoped they were going there. He couldn't have been happier as they steered that way.

They walked into the shade under the wide, corrugated metal wing. Mitch left his bicycle against the landing gear. Cornelius found a pair of sunglasses and slipped them on. Yuri Gagarin stood at the door and let them enter. He couldn't hide how pleased he was. They sat down in a red vinyl booth. Between the pepper and saltshakers and the ketchup, a little juke box on the table played "In the Mood."

They were in the mood, but they would have to wait. When they looked around, they realized the waitress was occupied.

Mitch and Cornelius recognized the voice talking to her before they turned around. Monte Deuce was the late-night sound carried on a hundred transistors and car radios. "I hate to tell you this, doll-face, but Benny Goodman died a long time ago. You got to get rid of this idea you got going in here. What is this place supposed to be? And what am I listening to? You got to get hip to the new sound! Howlin Wolf, Gene Vincent, Muddy Waters, Presley and the mystery train. That's only the beginning! Man! This nowheresville has got to go."

The waitress took her time asking him, "Are you going to criticize, or order breakfast?"

"Yeah, I'll order breakfast…You got bread and a toaster of some kind?"

She didn't say anything. Her hand remained frozen above the ticket pad.

"Okay, then I'd like a side-order of wheat toast."

She said, "We don't have side-orders. We only have what's on the menu."

"What do you mean?"

Mitch took a deep breath. An omelet was starting to burn.

The waitress repeated, "No side-orders."

He held out his hand. It was shining with rings. "Okay, I'll make it easy for you as I can. I'd like a chicken salad sandwich on wheat toast. Then push the chicken off the bread, butter it and—"

"Listen, mister. I've heard this routine before. I don't need it. You'll have to leave. I'm not taking any more of your smartness and sarcasm!"

Unfazed, Monte Deuce said blankly, "You like magic?" Then he slowly reached for his glass and smoothly tossed the water into the table speaker. A loud crackling and flash and Glenn Miller short circuited into smoke again. The smoke cleared, the waitress waved a towel at the air and Monte Deuce made his departure.

The cook shoved his head through the order window and barked from the kitchen, "What's going on out there?"

"Nothing!"

"What's burning?"

"The Glenn Miller Orchestra!" she called back. Waving the towel was managing to clear the smoke. She glanced at her three new customers. They were very quiet. "Sorry about that. That joker plays a few records for the teenagers and he thinks he's the new Pied Piper. He's paying for that juke next time he comes in. My hand to God, I don't put up with sass." She drew a line across the current page on her ticket pad and asked them, "Do you know what you'd like?" She quickly added, "No side-orders though!"

She felt instantly better when Yuri smiled at her. She knew him, she forgot everything bad, and she laughed when he pointed at the pictures on the menu. His glove jabbed every single one.

V.
The RED SEA

They couldn't walk past Rocket Market without Yuri tugging on Barter's sleeve. There was serious gravity going on. Even after consuming the entire right side of the Tin Goose menu, he couldn't resist the lure of the convenience store. "Yeah…alright…" Cornelius said. This Russian was costing him money, but he was about to make it all back. That cosmonaut was like one of the lucky stars that ride along your ship in deep space when you're lost, and they safely guide you to your destination.

"Cornelius Barter!" Digby LeStac greeted him from the counter. "Am I glad to see you."

"Really? Why's that?"

"Have you heard the radio today? KGUS has been hitting my new record every half hour. Deuce told me he sent copies to management in L.A. and New York. It's taking off!"

Cornelius nodded, "Hey, that's great."

Yuri was gathering another meal while Digby asked Cornelius if he could play trumpet for a recording. All Cornelius needed to hear was the pay.

"My shift is done at 2 o'clock. Can you meet me at The Red Sea? The sound in there is out of sight."

"Yeah, yeah, okay. I'll bring my horn."

Digby laughed as Yuri brought two stacked paper plates to the counter. "You going to a picnic?"

But Digby barely heard Cornelius respond, "I don't know. This cat never stops eating."

Digby LeStac had a deep well in his heart where he kept Carmen locked away like Rapunzel. He used to play the Carter Family for her, and he would put on records and dance with her. He remembered that place he rested his hand, just above her hip.

Outside the sun was shining, a blue sky was coming in like a tide pushing the clouds further north. Yuri had one plate balanced on top the other so he could eat using his left hand. He needed the energy to keep pleasing the people he met. Everyone at the Tin Goose had cheered him on, the cook left the kitchen to congratulate him, and the applause carried him out the door.

Mitch Itchmay had seen fame before, but nothing like that. Everyone seemed to think his 7th grade teacher was the greatest person in the world. He didn't get a chance to say goodbye, she was surrounded. He rode off on his bicycle to find somewhere he could draw.

"Man," Cornelius told Yuri, "You're something else." They crossed the street to the park and walked over the grass to a bench. The cover of a Cornelius Barter record ("Daybreak" on the SleepLess label) shows him sitting on that same bench. There was no plaque next to it, plaques and statues were for diplomats and soldiers. Anyone could sit on that bench and have their photo taken, the bench belonged to everyone. You could rest and never know Cornelius Barter and Yuri Gagarin had been there. Nobody took a picture of them, but someone was watching through binoculars, from behind a tree.

Pestus Cleek was determined this time. He shadowed Cornelius Barter—who wasn't dead—and his two companions, from the woods to the diner where he waited behind a parked car for them to be done. He was shocked by the way everyone cheered for the Russian and gathered around him like friends. They didn't know the first thing about treachery. Pestus was anxious, this situation was just like one of those science fiction Saturday matinees. Cleek was the only one who knew the truth and he couldn't get anyone to believe. So Pestus followed them to the park and watched the Russian eat hamburgers and he waited for his chance to strike. He was good at lurking.

It didn't take long before Yuri folded up his two empty paper plates and tossed them in the garbage can. He grinned, satisfied for now, sat back and watched two kids playing ball. He clapped his big gloves together as the girl jumped for a catch. He waved when they looked over at him.

Cornelius was only barely aware as Yuri left the bench and joined the game. Cornelius heard them laugh. He wondered what they were talking about, throwing the ball back and forth. They seemed to get along fine without words. Then he lay down, with his trumpet case as a pillow, and when he opened his eyes again the kids were gone. So was Yuri.

What time was it? Time never stopped running.

He sat up and the park spun. Objects orbited the bench: trees, dandelions, someone flying a kite, a flock of birds. He looked around and couldn't see the cosmonaut. A girl rode past on a bicycle. That's how it was with Cornelius Barter; things came and went. He stood, grabbed his trumpet and set off for the Red Sea.

He made it to the club two hours late. That wasn't bad. There were some gigs he never made it to at all. And ones where he arrived, but was only there as a ghost, slumped in a chair. This time wasn't like that. He gave Digby LeStac a solo beautiful as African flowers dotted with rain and he played three ballads too.

All that was hours from the sunny bench where he fell asleep, while Yuri Gagarin threw the ball back and forth with two happy children and Pestus Cleek began to creep. The wheels of the cart he pushed squeaked and the equipment stored in it rattled. As he neared their game, he whetted his lips and croaked, "Hotdogs…Hotdogs," a little louder each time. He took one last glance to make sure the jazz musician was good as dead. Cleek was pleased with his plan unreeling. The vendor stood by a tree, still counting the money he made to loan the cart. "Hotdogs," Pestus crooned.

The ball rolled in the grass and stopped.

It was the perfect fishing bait for a cosmonaut. Lures and spinners, soft plastic worms, and handmade fishing flies tied with red parade silk thread wouldn't do. Better than a shining star tugged on a hundred pound test line through the grass, the hotdog cart had done the trick.

Yuri Gagarin followed the cart out of the park, across streets, down sidewalk blocks, past houses and parked cars. Cleek lured him like an animal into the backyard of a cedar shake house, over to a table covered with birdhouses. The paint on them was still drying.

Pestus stopped the cart at the picnic table and opened a steaming lid. "You're hungry, aren't you?" He motioned for the hypnotized Russian to take a seat, then he got a hotdog. "Hamburgers, baseball and hotdogs…You're really enjoying our American way of life, aren't you?" He loaded the plate with another three hotdogs. "You want more? You do, don't you?

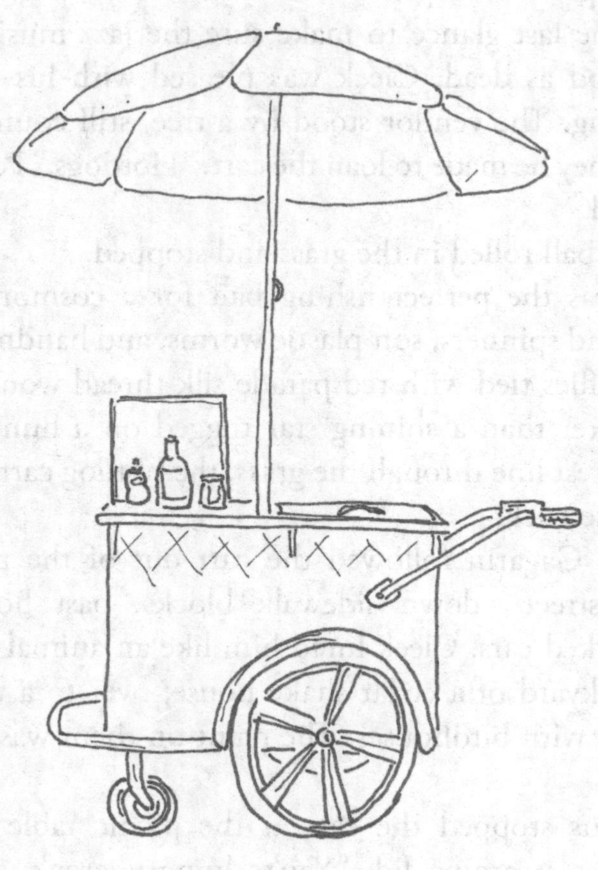

a real live invader

I bet you want this whole entire town and every good citizen in it." He stacked more on the plate. "But you and your comrades won't stop there, will you? It's never enough, is it?" He held the plate and sneered, "Here…You wait here and eat…I'll be right back."

He hurried to the house, opened the door and entered a hall. His shoes clacked like hooves as he rushed to the basement door. A wooden sign swung from a twine. Letters and numbers were burned into it: Troop 4109. Down the stairs an orange light glowed and the chatter of scouts busy tying knots. Pestus Cleek clattered on the steps. He had seen enough of those double features at Peoples to know the authorities were always shown up by a pack of courageous kids. If the police wouldn't listen to his story, they would when Troop 4109 delivered a bound and tethered communist to the desk clerk at the station.

The basement was the perfect command center, there were flags on the wall, tools on nails, a bobcat skin, a pinned map of the city, and eleven pairs of alerted eyes. Scout Master Evans stared at Pestus Cleek too.

When Cleek explained everything he had seen and how there was a real live invader in their neighborhood and that he needed their help capturing a Russian, what could they do? It was easy for kids to picture enemies dropping like bombs from the sky. Mr. Evans had to calm everyone down. He had a whistle around his neck but that was only for emergencies.

They followed Cleek back upstairs single file and down the echoey hall. Cleek was ahead of them, fumbling with the door. His first look out the window told him he was in trouble again. The hotdog cart was there, the lids were thrown open and a wisp of steam still escaped, but Yuri Gagarin's seat was empty.

A jet chalked across the blue sky.

The cosmonaut ate everything he could and then he left. Why hang around? His mission was to explore the rest of the day and into the night. That's where he went.

Like a black and white cowboy on Peoples' big screen, it was up to Cleek to pick up the pieces and deliver stirring words that would take them after their prey. He got a rousing cheer. They checked the rhododendron and the prickly junipers. They marched around the block looking everywhere. There wasn't much of a trail. And after an hour, you couldn't count on those kids anymore; their parents were arriving along the street and it was time for them to go home. Pestus Cleek was alone. He wanted to fight the dusk but he couldn't. It was leaning down on him heavier and heavier. If he was the only one to save America, then so be it.

The frogs were chirping as the moon rose and

shined on the ponds by the field.

When Cornelius Barter left the Red Sea, the music was still in his head and the street was dark. Polaris the North Star pointed the way.

VI.
CHICKEN LITTLE

Other worlds are part of ours, it's no secret. There are plenty of examples dropped here and there. What about Cornelius Barter's chair? Take a close look. How could a padded armchair sitting outside, exposed to the winter and rainy months of a Pacific Northwest spring not be turned into a soggy mound? The answer is simple. That fabric and frame is not of this planet. It came from LZU993 where rocking chairs swing from trees and sofas swim in lakes. Chairs like Barter's start as seeds blown like dandelion parachutes. If they get high enough, they can hitch a ride on the back of a shooting star. Earth waits at the end of a long commuter ride. There are even stones from YIT812 that traveled here as meteorites. People have picked them up before—off a rocky beach, or from the side of a road—but how many know to draw with them? From time to time a child will scratch a loop around a bug on the sidewalk and see it disappear. But how many know what sort of power they hold? Likewise if someone owns a chair for thirty years and it never seems to wear or fade in color, the owner will glow, "They don't make them like this anymore." Cornelius Barter never seemed to question his chair—it was just there, the way it always was. It radiated its own atmosphere—so when it rained, he never got wet, and if it snowed, he was never cold. It took care of him. It liked him. It kept the sunlight off his face so he could sleep late in the morning the next day.

Pestus Cleek was still looking for the cosmonaut. How was it possible for a man in a bright orange flight suit to hide? Cleek searched the neighborhood and finally stopped at the fence to look into Barter's yard. The trumpet player slept in the same deathly posture. No spaceship though. Cleek moved on. Some other rube could have taken the Russian in for the night, he seemed to have that power over people to delude their minds. It was also possible the cosmonaut had crawled into a garage like a stray dog. There were plenty of places to disappear.

Cleek thought of the deer that wandered through town. They could slip through fencing, cross backyards and cement as easily as phantoms, coming and going like mysterious unicorns. They melted into the overgrown field and stood still as trees, so why couldn't the cosmonaut stay camouflaged that same way? Surely their survival training included making a leafy burrow and lying low.

The day didn't seem to know the seriousness of Cleek's mission—the sky was clear and blue, birds were singing and playing in the branches—this day should have been gloomy gray like a midnight movie.

Spring was in full bloom like a parade.

It was hard to know exactly what Cleek was looking for: a little campfire and a balalaika song? He hoped the scouts were searching too. He left orders for them to. Or was this a school day? That shouldn't matter to a scout, he thought, they ought to climb that silver schoolyard fence and spread out.

The dirt path took him between a thicket of alders and then he was in the field. Surveying the shallow sea of yellow and green weeds, Cleek spotted an approaching figure. It never occurred to him what he was supposed to do if he met the Russian one-on-one. The field wouldn't be much of a Roman arena, all he had for a weapon was a whistle he could blow. Luckily as the person neared, Cleek could tell it was a white-haired woman, bundled in an overcoat, wearing a bright red lipstick smile. She waved. He did too, reluctantly.

She ambled along. She held some yellow flowers.

Pestus Cleek stood his ground and waited.

"Do you know who owns this field?" she asked when she was near.

He paused. He never thought about that. He was going to tell her it belongs to God, but he seemed to recall a sign that used to hang by the road years ago, "I think it's a church."

"It's such a nice place to walk," she continued.

He felt forced to agree.

A breeze ruffled the treetops. "I'm a little worried because I saw some lines and letters painted on the ground back there…"

"Oh," Cleek sighed, "Probably just an artist. They come here to paint still lifes and such."

As if she was already a statue, she raised her arm, puffed and declared, "The city should make this a park." She would go to city hall, she would make them know this place had worth beyond real estate. Enough people gathered together could do great things.

"Listen," Cleek said, "have you seen anyone suspicious around here?" and just like that, the woman realized there was something wrong. His words tumbled, "I'm looking for a potentially dangerous character."

She was speechless now. If only the flowers she held were the strings tied to a hundred balloons, enough to carry her free from him.

"If you see anyone in an orange spacesuit, alert the authorities." With that warning, Pestus Cleek set off again. There was no point going where she came from if she didn't see anyone. He tried a different path worn into the grass. The route took him into more brush and a stand of trees—no sign of a cosmonaut—twinkling scraps of litter packaging, a few empty bottles and cans…before the trail dropped him into the parking lot of Rocket Market.

Benton's car was gone. Cleek didn't want to ask Digby LeStac for help. He couldn't call the police again either.

Some kids arrived on skidding bicycles and leaned them by the glass door and flurried inside.

They made him think of Troop 4109 and Pestus went to the payphone and he would have dialed their number and got no answer at their headquarters, and he wouldn't have known who to call next. He needed a clairvoyant, a bloodhound, a conjurer. He could have tried the heavy thick phonebook hanging by a metal cord if he knew what to look for. Luckily, he didn't have to look far. The phone booth wall was a sort of message board, covered with graffiti and torn notices: music lessons, lost pets, get rich quick schemes. Then a business card caught his eye. It was calling him. Whatever it meant, it was singing for him. When he pulled it free, it was like picking a feather off a molting bird.

```
THE GREAT COLONEL MARCONI
          ???
    Making Magic Happen
          ???
  Promotions and Management
```

73

A phone number was printed in blue ink.

What did he have to lose?

He needed some magic to happen. A long night was gone and morning was crawling along with no luck. Cleek took out his coin purse and got a quarter.

Why not?

He dropped the coin into the slot and brought the receiver to his ear. The phone hummed with life as he dialed the numbers. After ten rings Cleek was still waiting, patient as someone fishing with a telephone line.

Then it happened, "Salutations!"

Cleek twitched and looked at the script on the card, "Is this Mr. Marconi?"

The leathery voice corrected him, "The *Great Colonel* Marconi."

"Is it true you can make magic happen?"

"That is my lot in life."

Cleek trusted the weary answer. "I need help finding someone."

Marconi chuckled, "I'm not running a Miss Lonelyhearts service, you know."

"No," Cleek flustered, "No, it's not that...I'm trying to find..." he faltered then sputtered, "Nobody believes what I've seen. Nobody understands what we're dealing with, and I lost track of what I'm looking for and now it's like I'm chasing a *ghost*."

"Aha!" Marconi exclaimed, "Now there's a word I'm familiar with! Yes, my partner and I have had great success in that area, but I'm not necessarily in that line of work anymore. You see, I'm retired." He lifted the kitchen curtain and gazed into the backyard. The lawn out there was pinned with croquet wickets. A big silver robot shined in the sunlight. It held a mallet with a clawed hand. "In fact, I'm rather busy at the moment, I have to get back to my game. If I'm not watching my partner, he tends to cheat."

Pestus Cleek tried to convince the old man, but it was no use. This was a test for Pestus Cleek. Like Job or Jonah or even that maniac jazz trumpet player, Cornelius Barter: finding that communist was Cleek's cross to bear. He hung up the phone and turned around.

Sighing, he looked at the sky. If there was a face up there in the clouds watching him, he wouldn't be surprised.

Close by, Mitch Itchmay stood in the empty parking spot with his notebook open. His eyes were narrowed in concentration as he drew.

Cleek knew he was on that page; he just knew he would be in the next newspaper edition, and it wouldn't be for catching a space invader. He knew he would be a cartoon. Cleek was right about that too.

Itchmay scratched a caricature of Chicken Little.

VII.
FIELD THEORY

exploring America

Two days and nights passed.

Songs were moved through the atmosphere: *Out of Nowhere, My Funny Valentine, I Remember You, Naima, Lady Bird, If You Could See Me Now, Morning Blues, September Song, But Beautiful, Solar.*

Cornelius Barter wondered where the spaceman was, where the spaceship went, and where he could find another trailer to park on the weedy lot. The chair from YIT812 tried its best, but it wasn't a bed. As he stirred, the shade began to fade and he realized it was another day.

Yuri Gagarin was taking his time exploring America. Some of the stories he heard were true, some of the things he saw confirmed what the Kremlin told them, but mostly he was amazed. Wherever he went, the people treated him like a long-lost friend. He played chess in the park, he fished off a dock, he went for a ride in a Cadillac. He was served like a king at the Fat Boy Drive-In. He stopped near a garage and heard teenagers playing their first racket of rock n roll, far from the music on the radio. Yuri was free. The night fell gentle as the one on Mars. A girl took him to the movies and held his arm. He had been in space for so long, he wanted to meet everyone. Some ran up to him in tears, other places there were cheers. Like the chameleons of Z421, he was adapting. People saw him how they wanted to see him; his smile meant everything.

Soon, he and Cornelius would just miss each other. There are orbits all through outer space where if you face the wrong way, or stoop to pet a meowing strawberry flower, you have lost your chance to see what goes flying by.

The teeth of a fern combed the trumpet case held by Barter's side. That trumpet meant everything to him. Though sometimes he would hock it for Green 17, it would always come back. Without music Cornelius Barter would be forgotten. Finches, sparrows, chickadees, balanced above him and sang in the trees. The field was ahead of him.

You could feel it was near. It was a wild space with no houses or roads, only those narrow padded trails shared with the deer. With no wires running overhead, at midnight you could stand in the middle of the field and watch the stars.

Cornelius walked past a tent planted thirty feet from the path. The trailer was only a step up from this. And now it was flattened and flown. He needed another one. Like most things with Cornelius Barter, it wasn't going to bug him, he could let it find him.

He smelled smoke and looked for the little

campfire, hoping someone had a hot tin of coffee to share. He shadowed his eyes with his hand and surveyed the field. In the south end where the land dipped into wetlands, he saw a coil of bluish smoke. That was alright. He guessed he knew who was there.

In another minute he was sitting with the fortune teller Countess Netinkama. A small fire was crackling before their feet. She leaned forward and poured him the cup he'd been wishing for. Every time he met her, she would take him into her imagination, the way a good patch of music would send him way out.

She said, "You see that hill?"

He took a sip and looked.

"On the other side is a circus. They got here very late last night. They're still sleeping. But someone left the lion cage open."

"What?" Cornelius drawled.

She nodded, "It's true."

"You—You don't seem too worried."

"No," she shook her head, "A lion is not the main danger to this field. I see greater misfortune ahead. The way you walked here was through a beautiful space. Others will be arriving, wearing yellow hardhats, surveying with measuring tapes and theodolite. They will pound stakes and paint lines across the grass and flowers. They will cause great harm. The rain will not enter the soil, the creek will be gone, the trees and the animals will be replaced by the walls they build."

Cornelius had never known her to be wrong, but he persisted, "But that's just…like a bad dream. It doesn't have to be that way."

"It's a possibility, a probability, maybe it's predictable, maybe not. Maybe it's a short circuit in my crystal ball. I hope that's all."

She let the fire die down while they had their coffee. Cornelius saw her red pickup truck backed up, surrounded by leaves. It had a wooden cabin grown to it like a snail shell. She would travel about town and beyond; sometimes she was here, sometimes she was gone. They both obeyed the same wind. When she asked him for a song, he got his trumpet and he was surprised to find "The Girl from Greenland." It was an old tune he played in Paris. No coyotes made a sound, but they must have been listening.

While Yuri Gagarin waited to cross Taylor Avenue, he just missed the song. A loud dairy truck rumble ran over the last note. By the time he reached the gravel path under the trees, the field had gone back to usual.

It was time for the cosmonaut to return to the spacecraft. He wasn't ready to leave, he just had to make sure that invisible pocket of air was still there. He could check the shortwave radio, press a few switches. He had two days' worth of logbook to write. As he waded into the field, he wondered what his superiors would think of his time in America. Would *Pravda* publish it?

One of the great pleasures of being on Earth is standing in a field, tilted to the sun. Yuri closed his eyes and listened. Far above him he heard a distant shrill cackle and opened his eyes and checked the blue sky. An eagle drifted in a slow arc. Up higher was another one circling. He counted five of them swirling at different heights. They were hunting. He knew they could see the writing on his flight jacket. He doubted they could read Russian though. Would they know he was a flier like them? He missed being up that high and he stared with his hand over his eyes remembering when he started out, piloting a Yak-18.

Cornelius Barter left towards the fortune teller's truck. Her name was painted on the side, with flowers and vines, birds and stars. He whispered something and snapped his fingers. He meant to ask her if she knew where he could get a trailer. The truck she had was a good setup—he could drive one to gigs—but it was no Jaguar Type E. No, he decided against it. Trucks like these used to die in the dust from Oklahoma to California. A block of firewood was propped against a wheel, and in the shadows underneath her truck, a drowsy lion was watching him.

VIII.
The SONG

Pestus Cleek wasn't giving up. After half a week of searching for the cosmonaut, he was on the third floor of the *Herald* building, talking through a window cut in the wall. The receptionist couldn't believe the timing—Cleek arrived just as his song was playing on the radio.

"This has got to be considered newsworthy!" he bleated. "I saw it with my own eyes."

"I know, you already said. A sputnik landed in someone's backyard."

"No, not a sputnik! This had a pilot in it. Now he's walking around town, free as a bird. People need to know, the police need to arrest him."

She reached her arm over towards the transistor radio, but not to turn it off. She tapped her cigarette in the ashtray. She murmured along with the catchy lyrics. She could have sung it by heart by now. So could most people in town.

Cleek seethed, "Is it possible for you to dim that contraption. That song follows me wherever I go! I hate it! Wouldn't you think there would be a way to ban it?"

She turned the dial, but she couldn't help repeating the cheerful refrain, "Oh Pestus Cleek, what's the

a full-fledged invasion

matter with you?"

"That's just it! Nothing's the matter with *me*, thank you very much. The real question is, what's the matter with everyone else? Why won't anyone listen? Does *nobody else* see what's going on? It's a full-fledged invasion!"

"I realize, Mr. Cleek." She took a breath of cigarette and the smoke released as she spoke. "But you've got no evidence. Do you have a photograph? Or a plaster casting?"

"It's not the Loch Ness Monster we're talking about!"

"Tell you what—since it's so important—why don't you write a letter to the editor? There's paper on the counter over there, and a pencil, and when you're done you can drop it in the suggestion box."

"Don't you have a spare reporter I can talk to?" The room behind her was full of typewriters at tables and stacks of overflowing paper, but no other employees in sight.

"Mr. Cleek, if you'll just write your story, someone will be sure to read it." She returned to her cigarette.

He wanted to say more but she was hidden in a cloud. "At least I can count on the young people of today. My scouts have been hunting two days for that communist invader."

"Troop 4109?" she guessed.

"Yes…"

"They're downstairs. They're working on the parade."

"Parade?"

"Oh, Mr. Cleek, haven't you seen today's *Herald*? It's on the front page."

"No, I've been too busy trying to get *my* story on the front page."

"Well, there's a paper in the vending machine on your way out." She pointed with her cigarette, "Don't forget to fill out your letter to the editor. You'll feel better." Then she returned to the pile in front of her. She was done with Cleek…until the next time his song played on the radio.

Pestus Cleek understood he was getting the runaround. As usual, it was him against the world.

Suite 301 surrounded with wood paneled walls. A section was peeling down from the ceiling. He could see the tobacco colored original wall. Once there was a cloud layer that never left up there. Once this room was bustling. Now there were three chairs on a carpeted floor with a counter to lean on. A coffee can sat on the counter.

Taped to it was a handwritten sign: SUGGESTIONS. He tore a page off the notebook pad and used his own pen to write:

The Editor
The Herald

Dear Sir,

A few nights ago, I became aware that we have been invaded by Russian spacemen. I dutifully alerted the authorities, but the police were too late and the situation has only grown in urgency day by day. I'm doing my part as a citizen, but it is high time the authorities do something about it.

Sincerely
P. Cleek

He folded the page twice, running a fingernail firmly along the seam so it was a neat square, then he dropped it through a slot in the can. It splashed like a penny in a wishing well. If they published his warning tomorrow, that would get the ball rolling. The lady in the window was gone now. Not even a smoke cloud.

On his way to the elevator, he passed the vending machine. He stooped to examine the front page. PROTESTERS HAVE FIELD DAY. It would cost a dime to read the rest of the story.

Across from the *Herald* building, up Chestnut

Street a block or two, Yuri Gagarin was following the alleys downhill. He never seemed to tire, but he was, and he was hungry again too. By now he knew all he had to do was stop at the alley door of a restaurant and wait there like a monk with an empty bowl. The moment someone saw him, the dishwasher or the cook, they would rejoice and bring him plates of food. Once he got downtown there were cafés on every corner. The smell of another one was near and his charm had no end.

In outer space on those lonely unpaved roads, you don't meet many travelers and the sight of the two merging in front of him slowed Yuri to a halt. An old man wearing a tuxedo and a top hat and leaning on a cane and looking like he just unfolded from a steamer trunk was unusual enough, but next to him was a silver robot, seven feet tall.

After years of magic, Marconi stayed prepared for the sleight of hand, but when he spotted the man in the orange spacesuit, he reached for his friend's metal arm. It was more than a chrysanthemum popping into view. "Cronco!" the old man croaked, "What is this apparition?"

The robot's meters and dials spun and clicked as the air was measured.

Then right before Marconi's astonished eyes, the cosmonaut became someone he knew. It was instant illusion, done so deftly Marconi was truly fooled. "Lloyd?" he gasped. "Lloyd, is that you?" Marconi beamed and chattered, "Well, well, well! Hello Lefty! I haven't seen you since Luna Park! Then I heard you died. Apparently not! Gee it's good to see you. How are you?"

Cronco intervened, reading the cosmonaut's smile and thoughts and carrying them back and forth. "He says, *I came on a ship*."

Marconi looked confused, "What ship? Down at the harbor?"

Cronco whirled and replied, "*I came from the sky*."

"What's that?" Marconi stared at the expressionless robot, "What's that mean? An airplane?"

"The picture he is transmitting is that of a rocket."

Marconi gasped, "Lefty Doolan driving a rocket ship? Preposterous! I don't think so."

The robot said, "You are correct. This is not Lloyd Doolan. My sensors indicate this is—"

But that was as far as Cronco got. The cosmonaut was a breeze.

The Marcels sang "Blue Moon" on a record player above the alley in a shuttered room. It was the number one single in America.

IX.
CIRCUS PEOPLE

Mitch Itchmay drew a picture of Cornelius Barter up a tree, with a lion below him.

The lion sat by the trunk, paws crossed, like someone waiting at a Paris café. It yawned sharp teeth and lifted its shaggy head to blink at the trumpet player above.

"Maybe you could play him a lullaby," Mitch suggested.

"Man, I'm hanging on for my life!" A leaf let go and slowly parachuted. "Why doesn't he try eating you? There's a lot more meat on you."

Mitch shrugged. He sat on a stump not ten feet from the lion, calmly drawing. "I guess you just caught his eye." He switched pens to draw the fine lines of the weeds. "You know what? This should be the cover for your next album."

The lion snapped at the leaf. That was just an hors d'oeuvre.

"My last album," Cornelius said.

"Nawww," said Mitch. "Nettie will be back any minute with the trainer. Any sign of them from up there?"

"All I can see are trees."

In a moment, Mitch said, "What if you sang to

the lion?"

"Mitch…" Cornelius sighed, "This is not the time for music."

That didn't stop Mitch who crooned out of tune, "Moon shining down on some little town…and with each beam, same old dream."

A crow seemed to laugh from another treetop.

"Stick to your drawing, Mitch," Cornelius advised.

Mitch swatted a mosquito on his bare leg. "How'd you get up that tree so fast?"

"When there's a lion after you, you climb."

"Well, I don't know. I don't think you have to worry. He's doesn't look that hungry. I think he's just a fan."

Cornelius wasn't about to take that chance. Up a tree, he wasn't much more than skin, bones, muscle and songs that would float free of him like a bird. "I hear something," he called down. A rumble of engines. "I see them."

Mitch heard them too. He closed the notebook. He got everything he needed. The crow, his appreciative audience, took to wing. Then he saw the circus arriving.

A big orange truck, followed by a slow procession of others, bounced and rocked in the lane where the Countess had parked. Branches squeaked and scraped.

Cornelius looked through the leaves. "I didn't

expect her to bring the whole Saturn Circus!"

The row of vehicles came to rest like elephants in the jungle.

The lion wasn't concerned. The dappling light under the tree blinked on his yellow fur like sunbeams in a stream.

The big truck in the lead snorted and as the motor died, the doors on either side opened. Mitch waved to the Countess Netinkama and the driver. More circus people were emerging alongside. Mitch opened his notebook again.

Cornelius Barter waited until the lion was leashed before he started to descend. The next time he would be climbing the tree it would be evening and he would be up there to play a song, with lanterns hung around him from the branches. By then he wouldn't be afraid of the lion, it was just like Mitch said—he had a fan. That lion just wanted to be by his side.

Cornelius had another admirer as he climbed down and reached the ground and heard his name said next to him.

"It's been a while," she continued.

There were carriages with animals and trucks unloading canvas. Someone was leading the lion into the field. It took a long five seconds for time to unfold and for him to say her name. He said he couldn't believe it was her, he felt like he walked out of an elevator.

On the other side of the field, down Garden Street, a parade was just turning off East Chestnut. The high school marching band blasted away. Troop 4109 came after them, and there were signs held in the air like, SAVE THE FIELD, and OUR SPACE STAYS. The cherry trees were still in blossom. The *Herald* had three reporters covering it.

As the current pushed uphill, Marconi and Cronco joined in. Wheezing and creaking, the old magician and the robot slowly fell towards the end with the baby strollers. Cronco's silver metal sent flashes from back there.

Digby LeStac saw all the people walking by his job at Rocket Market and he hopped around the counter and ran to the door. It was like the *USS St. Francis* steaming by. In another minute he put a CLOSED sign on the window, grabbed his guitar and locked the store.

Benton, sleeping in his apartment, missed the whole thing.

By the end of the day Mitch Itchmay would fill his notebook.

Just past Maple Street, Pestus Cleek caught a glimpse of an orange spacesuit next to a parked car. "Ahah!" he couldn't help shouting. After all that tracking, it was momentous as finding Amelia Earhart.

Yuri Gagarin turned toward the shout, while the sound of the parade was coming their way, and he became a man wearing a blue military uniform. General Ulysses S. Grant standing beside a Buick Skylark.

With the steely eyes regarding him, Cleek felt his knees buckle. He waited all his life to faint in ecstasy on a patch of dandelions beside a No Parking sign.

After that, Yuri Gagarin was exhausted. It was tiring changing back and forth, back and forth. He couldn't do it anymore. The past few days and nights caught up with him. Waves had knocked him over, again and again. He was fascinated by America, but it wore him out, it was time to get back to the solitude of his Vostok. If only he could make it there unseen.

An alley ran between Garden and High Street. He could spy far enough ahead, if someone else was coming, he would duck into the shadows. Over the rows of houses and trees and apartments blared the marching band and the echoes of the crowd. Like May Day on the radio, the sound had a life of its own. He was carried along in the airwaves.

He remembered Russia.

He was a hero, an international star.

They put his face on a postage stamp.

That's where the Cosmonaut Training Centre wanted to keep him, glued down. They had to keep him in sight on the ground. They only let Yuri Gagarin fly ten hours during 1968. Everyone who knew him knew that he lived to fly. He had been the first person to travel in space, but Star City made sure he couldn't get airborne again. He never stopped trying though, begging them over and over until finally they allowed him half an hour in a MiG-15 trainer…with a flight instructor in the backseat…in the freezing March rain. They didn't want him to enjoy flying, they wanted him to be miserable. They made it difficult. He got the wrong weather report, and he would find the old jet had an altimeter that would fail in a dive. The plane had been overhauled six times since it was built in 1956. But as it lifted off the murky gray runway, Yuri was smiling. The roar in his ears, the jumping needles in dials, the feeling of shooting ahead like an astronaut. "Poyekhali!" he hailed into the radio.

A break in the cloud layer showed snow below them. A second later, they were back in the clouds. Whatever it was that happened next was so quick he never knew the Earth was taken away from him.

Suddenly he appeared on OSA844. The air was heavy with ozone. He wore his orange cosmonaut flight suit, his boots were planted on a lily pad big as a round floor carpet. It held his weight as he walked across it to the next one, a little unsteadily to another. He was reminded of the Caspian Sea. He spotted something, a distant ball of reflecting light on the green horizon, shining like a city in Azerbaijan.

At some point, the lily pads had crawled up onto land and he was walking in a grassy field.

He wasn't aware of crossing Taylor Avenue, or the gravel track that took him to Cornelius Barter's. Ahead of him he saw the 1961 Vostok waiting for him, reflecting the two suns of OSA844. At the right spot, Yuri got his YIT812 dowsing stone and swept it over the ground until a path appeared. Around he went again, drawing the invisible curtain aside, making the spaceship reveal itself. The hatch was open.

It was dusk and the circus and all the people in the parade were filling up the nearby field. The cosmonaut could hear the welcome. He thought of Moscow's Red Square after he returned from orbit. He was his own circus and parade. He was part of an electricity Star City wanted to control like a kite, stringing him out. They sent him to Czechoslovakia, Bulgaria, Finland, Paris, London, Canada and south to open the Soviet-Cuban Friendship Society. Since 1961 he had been exploring other worlds. That was his role in life. He closed the hatch and prepared the ship for liftoff.

X.
RED ROSE

Night was falling. A crescent moon sawed in the sky. Candles and lanterns lined the deer path through the dark. The field had turned into Coney Island. The Saturn Circus and everyone else. Cornelius Barter promised an old friend he would play a song for her and he threaded the crowd towards the lion's tree. She would be up in the air listening and he wanted to be up there with her. He already had a good place in that tree. He passed the dim silhouette of a horse or a llama or a short giraffe. Trained dogs were running round a candlelit circle, jumping through a hoop. Spotlights hit an acrobat on a high-wire and he waved to her. Kids laughing, Digby LeStac strumming the guitar, and from another place came the sound of Bo Diddley.

As before, the Countess Netinkama sat in her chair. This time, instead of a fire, a tall lamp stood in the morning's ashes. She was reading a book by the light. A crystal ball and a deck of cards rested on the spindly table next to her. She could also see the future in palms and tea leaves. Her cup of Red Rose formed a picture of the field. For her it was real as a photograph.

Knowing he was near, she held her place in the book and called, "Cornelius, do you want your

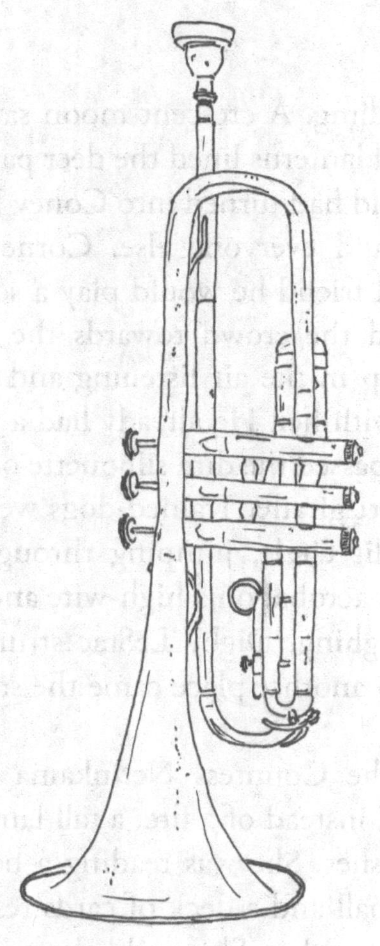

light was climbing

future read?"

"No, no thanks." He rested into the other chair next to her, "I'm only here while I'm here."

She refilled her cup and one for him too. They talked about the field.

The Countess admitted, "I'm pleased my second sight was wrong this time. Sometimes you imagine the worst and you really believe it's going to happen." Her bracelets rattled, "I'm glad I was wrong, but don't let the word get around." She took a sip and watched the tealeaves settle. "I heard you're going to play a song."

"The news travels fast."

In her cup she saw him at the top of the tree. The lion was back there too, listening. She heard Cornelius Barter play "I Get Along Without You Very Well" as a dot of diamond light was climbing through the leaves of the tree.

"Did you see that?" he interrupted her thought.

"What?"

He pointed, "I saw something in that tree. It was a little spark moving around like a firefly. I know we don't have those around here though."

She looked where he was pointing, a deep blue oak tree in silhouette. Then she nodded, "That's a fairy light. They only appear to those in a dire situation."

If Cornelius Barter had seen one before, he couldn't

remember, but he had been in plenty of dire situations. Maybe they hid in the taillights of a passing car in Sausalito. They could have watched him from the soot and neon pulsing in Times Square. He had chances galore to see those lights.

It drifted about purposefully like a spark. For a few seconds more it shined, then like a light bulb, it suddenly turned off. "That's all," she told him. "Every light, no matter how holy or not, ends the same way, like a candle going out." She finished her tea and looked back in her cup. The picture changed. Now he was singing the lyrics to a slow-moving rocket flame rising above the tree.

It looked like a firework, but Cornelius knew what it was and who was in that spaceship leaving Earth.

The lantern glow and the music and commotion that filled the field like the air in a balloon would be gone by morning. Coney Island would lift off and float somewhere else. Maybe all the way to RRL992. That blue planet could use it.

Yuri Gagarin knew there was a lot more to explore, there always was, but he only had a short time and so much to see. Above the parking lot of Rocket Market, the fiery dot moved with the moths ganged around the buzzing neon sign. The roar and g-force pinned him to his chair. He couldn't turn to look out the window if he tried. He would be missed. He would stay in their thoughts as a little torn memory, like a moment of film that could be put on a reel and spun again and again.

Midnight splashed against the window as the spaceship turned. He was in orbit. He felt his weight disappear. The porthole showed the darkest black and then became the sight of Earth curving into view. Oceans, mountains, forests and cities. His glove waved over the switch settings. When Yuri pressed the three numbered buttons on the keypad to his left—3-2-5—the ship was on auto-control, no meddling from Star City trying to bring him down. His Vostok broke orbit and aimed for outer space.

Being higher in the tree, Cornelius could see the spaceship a second longer than anyone else. His song ended with it blinking out and that would have been his lasting memory if it wasn't for the news that broke the next day.

XI.
MISSING PERSON

The *Herald* pushed the new park to the middle of page 4. This was one of those rare, historical days—a person had flown into space and back. Yuri Gagarin and his spacecraft fell on the outskirts of Smelkovka in a potato field and the news flashed around the world.

"That's him!" Cornelius told Mitch. He stamped the newspaper with his finger. "He's the cat who smashed my trailer. You know him too, remember?" He passed the paper to Mitch Itchmay.

"I don't know…"

"We had breakfast together! Remember all the food he ate?"

Mitch laughed, "That wasn't a cosmonaut, that was my seventh grade art teacher! I didn't want to make a scene, I tried to keep it together. I was just glad to see her again. She's the one who told me never stop drawing."

"What?—No! This is *him*. Look at him, look at that smile."

"I'm sorry, I don't know this guy. He's Russian! I don't know any Russians. How would I?"

Cornelius glared across the park.

"Look," Mitch said. He carried his notebook around the way Barter toted his horn. He flipped the pages until he found what he was looking for. "I drew this when we were at the diner."

"Oh, no…That's all wrong. You're not even close. I never saw her before."

"What do you mean? She was sitting right next to you."

Cornelius drummed his fingers on the trumpet case.

"I just figured you knew her," Mitch said. "You're both artists."

Cornelius stared at the gray photo on the front page. He knew that was his visitor, it wasn't a Green 17 delusion. The proof was the burned litter that used to be his trailer, the crater that was left behind where it was. But would anyone believe a Vostok rocket did that?

Pestus Cleek spent a week believing that, but after he woke up on the curb, woozy as a medieval saint knocked over by an angel, his life had a new purpose. This time he didn't bother with the police, he went straight to the *Herald*. He already knew the routine, he didn't bother the receptionist, he picked up a notecard and wrote:

The Editor
The Herald

Dear Sir,

Please disregard my previous letter. There's a matter of much more importance at hand. I would like to post a notice in your Missing Persons column. I am trying to find Ulysses S. Grant. I last saw him in the vicinity of Maple Street. Unfortunately, my overwhelmed faculties departed me and by the time I recovered he was nowhere to be found.
I greatly appreciate your help in this matter,

Sincerely
P. Cleek

p.s He was last seen wearing his Civil War general's uniform.

Meanwhile on a croquet course a mile away, Cronco interrupted The Great Colonel Marconi, "While you are lining up that shot, could you perhaps loan me some reading material to bide the time?"

Marconi broke concentration and groaned, "I nearly had it!" He took the crumpled roll of *Herald* from his tuxedo pocket and held it out for the waiting robot's claw. "Read to your heart's content. Meanwhile do me the justice of allowing me the peace to contemplate this difficult shot." He bent again and swung his mallet gently back.

Cronco shrilled like a factory whistle.

Marconi jumped and juggled his mallet. "What now?! Must you fault me with histrionics every time it's my turn?"

The steam that clouded over Cronco vaporized. He shook the front page. It was a wonder his oscillating grip didn't shred it into confetti. Agitated as he was, his voice maintained a steady monotone, "My sensors indicate we have met this cosmonaut."

"Your sensors…" Marconi grimaced.

"In the alley."

"You're telling me we met a Russian rocketeer in an alley?"

"Correct. He does appear to be the same illusion in question. Apparently only robots can see the situation for what it is—a mirage."

"How could it be? Have you lost your marbles?"

"I believe you incorrectly referred to him as Lefty."

Marconi puffed, "You think I don't know Lloyd Doolan when I see him?"

"I do not doubt what you think you saw. And yet Lloyd Doolan has been dead for thirty six years."

The old magician had to ponder that. He leaned on his mallet. Here they were playing croquet while another ghost was in their midst. "I suppose it's a strange detail that his manifestation was just the way I remembered him then."

"It is my deduction that we were contacted by an unusual alien life form, one that has the power to change appearance, to look into the minds of others and find a memory of someone dear."

"And for me it was my old partner," Marconi said. "Of course, I heard Lefty died long ago, but I wanted him to be alive. It was foolish of me to fall for that."

"No, not foolish," the robot told him, "Human. Your intention is quite simple to understand. All it takes is a basic—"

"Alright, Cronco!" Marconi waved his arm and there was an almost imperceptible click as his mallet absently tapped the red striped ball. He froze. He couldn't believe what he had done.

An airplane buzzed like a bumblebee overhead.

They both listened to it fade, then the robot made a show of neatly folding the newspaper before returning it to Marconi. The plane became a soft burr, barely heard.

With a calculated whir, Cronco's gleaming eyes returned to the game, "I believe it is my turn."

wobbling in the stars

A hundred miles high and climbing, Yuri Gagarin had one last look at our world, small, blue, wobbling in the stars and he spoke into the microphone, "Dear friends, both known and unknown to me, fellow countrymen, men and women of all lands and continents. In a moment, my spaceship will take me into the faraway expanses of the universe. I want to thank all of you for your faith in me and know that your memory of me will be my memory too. I say goodbye to you all, dear friends, and wish you all happiness." He was smiling as he set the coordinates for SFN88. There was nothing else to do but wait until he got there.

COSMONAUT

Writing by Allen Frost

during March—May 2021

From *Almost Animals*, painting by Laura Vasyutynska

Books by Good Deed Rain

Saint Lemonade, Allen Frost, 2014. Two novels illustrated by the author in the manner of the old Big Little Books.

Playground, Allen Frost, 2014. Poems collected from seven years of chapbooks.

Roosevelt, Allen Frost, 2015. A Pacific Northwest novel set in July, 1942, when a boy and a girl search for a missing elephant. Illustrated throughout by Fred Sodt.

5 Novels, Allen Frost, 2015. Novels written over five years, featuring circus giants, clockwork animals, detectives and time travelers.

The Sylvan Moore Show, Allen Frost, 2015. A short story omnibus of 193 stories written over 30 years.

Town in a Cloud, Allen Frost, 2015. A three part book of poetry, written during the Bellingham rainy seasons of fall, winter, and spring.

A Flutter of Birds Passing Through Heaven: A Tribute to Robert Sund, 2016. Edited by Allen Frost and Paul Piper. The story of a legendary Ish River poet & artist.

At the Edge of America, Allen Frost, 2016. Two novels in one book blend time travel in a mythical poetic America.

Lake Erie Submarine, Allen Frost, 2016. A two week vacation in Ohio inspired these poems, illustrated by the author.

and Light, Paul Piper, 2016. Poetry written over three years. Illustrated with watercolors by Penny Piper.

The Book of Ticks, Allen Frost, 2017. A giant collection of 8 mysterious adventures featuring Phil Ticks. Illustrated throughout by Aaron Gunderson.

I Can Only Imagine, Allen Frost, 2017. Five adventures of love and heartbreak dreamed in an imaginary world. Cover & color illustrations by Annabelle Barrett.

The Orphanage of Abandoned Teenagers, Allen Frost, 2017. A fictional guide for teens and their parents. Illustrated by the author.

In the Valley of Mystic Light: An Oral History of the Skagit Valley Arts Scene, 2017. A comprehensive illustrated tribute. Edited by Claire Swedberg & Rita Hupy.

Different Planet, Allen Frost, 2017. Four science fiction adventures: reincarnation, robots, talking animals, outer space and clones. Cover & illustrations by Laura Vasyutynska.

Go with the Flow: A Tribute to Clyde Sanborn, 2018. Edited by Allen Frost. The life and art of a timeless river poet. In beautiful living color!

Homeless Sutra, Allen Frost, 2018. Four stories: Sylvan Moore, a flying monk, a water salesman, and a guardian rabbit.

The Lake Walker, Allen Frost 2018. A little novel set in black and white like one of those old European movies about death and life.

A Hundred Dreams Ago, Allen Frost, 2018. A winter book of poetry and prose. Illustrated by Aaron Gunderson.

Almost Animals, Allen Frost, 2018. A collection of linked stories, thinking about what makes us animals.

The Robotic Age, Allen Frost, 2018. A vaudeville magician and his faithful robot track down ghosts. Illustrated throughout by Aaron Gunderson.

Kennedy, Allen Frost, 2018. This sequel to Roosevelt is a coming-of-age fable set during two weeks in 1962 in a mythical Kennedyland. Illustrated throughout by Fred Sodt.

Fable, Allen Frost, 2018. There's something going on in this country and I can best relate it in fable: the parable of the rabbits, a bedtime story, and the diary of our trip to Ohio.

Elbows & Knees: Essays & Plays, Allen Frost, 2018. A thrilling collection of writing about some of my favorite subjects, from B-movies to Brautigan.

The Last Paper Stars, Allen Frost 2019. A trip back in time to the 20 year old mind of Frankenstein, and two other worlds of the future.

Walt Amherst is Awake, Allen Frost, 2019. The dreamlife of an office worker. Illustrated throughout by Aaron Gunderson.

When You Smile You Let in Light, Allen Frost, 2019. An atomic love story written by a 23 year old.

Pinocchio in America, Allen Frost, 2019. After 82 years buried underground, Pinocchio returns to life behind a car repair shop in America.

Taking Her Sides on Immortality, Robert Huff, 2019. The long awaited poetry collection from a local, nationally renowned master of words.

Florida, Allen Frost, 2019. Three days in Florida turned into a book of sunshine inspired stories.

Blue Anthem Wailing, Allen Frost, 2019. My first novel written in college is an apocalyptic, Old Testament race through American shadows while Amelia Earhart flies overhead.

The Welfare Office, Allen Frost, 2019. The animals go in and out of the office, leaving these stories as footprints.

Island Air, Allen Frost, 2019. A detective novel featuring haiku, a lost library book and streetsongs.

Imaginary Someone, Allen Frost, 2020. A fictional memoir featuring 45 years of inspirations and obstacles in the life of a writer.

Violet of the Silent Movies, Allen Frost, 2020. A collection of starry-eyed short story poems, illustrated by the author.

The Tin Can Telephone, Allen Frost, 2020. A childhood memory novel set in 1975 Seattle, illustrated by author like a coloring book.

Heaven Crayon, Allen Frost, 2020. How the author's first book Ohio Trio would look if printed as a Big Little Book. Illustrated by the author.

Old Salt, Allen Frost, 2020. Authors of a fake novel get chased by tigers. Illustrations by the author.

A Field of Cabbages, Allen Frost, 2020. The sequel to The Robotic Age finds our heroes in a race against time to save Sunny Jim's ghost. Illustrated by Aaron Gunderson.

River Road, Allen Frost, 2020. A paperboy delivers the news to a ghost town. Illustrated by the author.

The Puttering Marvel, Allen Frost, 2021. Eleven short stories with illustrations by the author.

Something Bright, Allen Frost, 2021. 106 short story poems walking with you from winter into spring. Illustrated by the author.

The Trillium Witch, Allen Frost, 2021. A detective novel about witches in the Pacific Northwest rain. Illustrated by the author.

Cosmonaut, Allen Frost, 2021. Yuri Gagarin stars in this novel that follows his rocket landing in an American town. Midnight jazz, folk music, mystery and sorcery. Illustrated by the author.

∞

Loyal readers will recognize several returning characters in *Cosmonaut*. Cornelius Barter also appears in *5 Novels* and *Pinocchio in America*; Marconi and Cronco in *The Robotic Age* and *A Field of Cabbages*.

∞

Cover Artist, **Laura Vasyutynska** is an accomplished visual artist, experienced with both traditional and computer media, who has been pursuing a career as a professional artist since her youth, beginning formal training in her hometown of Zhytomyr, Ukraine. Laura moved to the United States in early 2001 and continued her career in Seattle, Washington. Recently graduated from the University of North Texas with a Master of Fine Arts in Drawing & Painting, she works primarily with oils on canvas, watercolors, ink and graphite, but also uses digital media. Much of her work is imaginative, and ventures from realistic subject matter to abstract. Her color sense is rich and vibrant, influenced by the folk patterns and decoration of her native country. Her artwork for Good Deed Rain includes: *Different Planet, Homeless Sutra, Almost Animals, Fable*, and *Cosmonaut.*

Author, **Allen Frost** has published poetry, short stories and novels, and is editor of Good Deed Rain books. Currently he can be seen walking his dog and taking notes under trees.